W9-AQC-120

RED DOG

Football Poems

BLUE FLY

By Sharon Bell Mathis

Pictures by
Jan Spivey Gilchrist

It's . . . that kind of season.
Eloise Greenfield

MOOSEHEART
ELEMENTARY
SCHOOL LIBRARY
60539

Viking

VIKING
Published by the Penguin Group
Viking Penguin, a division of Penguin Books USA Inc.,
375 Hudson Street, New York, New York 10014, U.S.A.
Penguin Books Ltd, 27 Wrights Lane, London W8 5TZ, England
Penguin Books Australia Ltd, Ringwood, Victoria, Australia
Penguin Books Canada Ltd, 2801 John Street, Markham, Ontario, Canada L3R 1B4
Penguin Books (N.Z.) Ltd, 182–190 Wairau Road, Auckland 10, New Zealand

Penguin Books Ltd, Registered Offices: Harmondsworth, Middlesex, England

First published in 1991 by Viking Penguin, a division of Penguin Books USA Inc.

1   3   5   7   9   10   8   6   4   2

Text copyright © Sharon Bell Mathis, 1991
Illustrations copyright © Jan Spivey Gilchrist, 1991
All rights reserved
Library of Congress Catalog Card Number: 91-50266
ISBN 0-670-83623-0
Printed in U.S.A.
Set in 14 point Egyptian 505
Without limiting the rights under copyright reserved above, no part of this
publication may be reproduced, stored in or introduced into a retrieval
system, or transmitted, in any form or by any means (electronic, mechanical,
photocopying, recording or otherwise), without the prior written permission
of both the copyright owner and the above publisher of this book.

The quote that appears on the title page is taken from *Under the
Sunday Tree*, by Eloise Greenfield, published by Harper & Row, 1988.

This book is for my two favorite tough guys

My Grandson: Thomas Kevin Allen, II
OXON HILL BOYS AND GIRLS CLUB

My Nephew: John W. Bell, III
CLINTON BOYS AND GIRLS CLUB

S.B.M.

For the Deans, Jenkins and Spivey Boys
and thanks to Morgan Lewis

J.S.G.

RED DOG/BLUE FLY

Signals signals hey

oh yeah

plays that say

go here—be there

signals red, signals blue

stuck up in my mind like glue

red dog/blue dog

signals for defense

trying to remember them

keeps me tense

red fly/blue fly

signals for offense

gotta keep them straight

so they make some sense

Coach yelling, "What I tell you
'bout your plays!"
and we keep on practicing
for days and days

Maybe it's easier to be a quitter
and hide out in my uncle's van
where I never have to understand
that red's not blue
and blue's not red
or that forgetting a signal
fills me with dread
red dog/blue fly
is a boogey-man
lullaby

FOOTBALL

You twist
right out my hand
and fly
into the air

I bend and
turn and
jump up high
but you don't seem to care

Pigskin rascal
never kind
too far in front
or way behind

You sail above my fingers
you sail above my head
why not sail
into my hands instead

Pigskin brat
mean and tough
you play too hard
you play too rough

COACH

OFFENSE
you run the ball straight
or parallel
touchdown
or field goal
do it well
OFFENSE—you ADVANCE the ball
it ain't complicated at all

DEFENSE
you gotta stay strong
make what they do
turn out wrong
it's as plain as 1, 2, 3
so—if a pass gets by
you gonna hear from me
DEFENSE—you STOP their ball
it ain't complicated at all

OFFENSE
DEFENSE
here's the deal
we can make winning—real

MONSTER MAN

One sack
two sacks
three sacks
four

Hands stinging
shoulders sore

Five sacks
six sacks
seven
eight

Quarterback's men
too late too late

Nine sacks
ten sacks
eleven
twelve

I'm a 70-pound hatchet
they just can't shelve

Call me mauler
call me whiz
my only job is
ruin his

QUARTERBACK

Something in my head
lights up
kicks in
and fires
the engine I have to be
it pushes signals out my mouth
focuses my eyes
I miss nothing
see everything
my arm
unlocks
becomes
a heart
pumping
an atom splitting
pile-driving
main frame
drum major

Randall Cunningham's arm
Warren Moon's arm
Rodney Peete's arm
Doug Williams' arm
I
hope

Cause if this machine misfires
my master chef
arm
overcooks
and burns not them—but us

TOUCHDOWN

Ball tight
against my chest
my skinny legs
try their best

Crafty weavers
in gold and blue
spin a hole
and I run through

Up ahead is all
I know
can't fall down
can't be slow

Defense diving
'round my feet
neither stop my time
nor match my beat

I cross the line
but cannot see
the upstretched arms
of the referee

I spike the ball
away from my chest
and salute my skinny legs
for doing their best

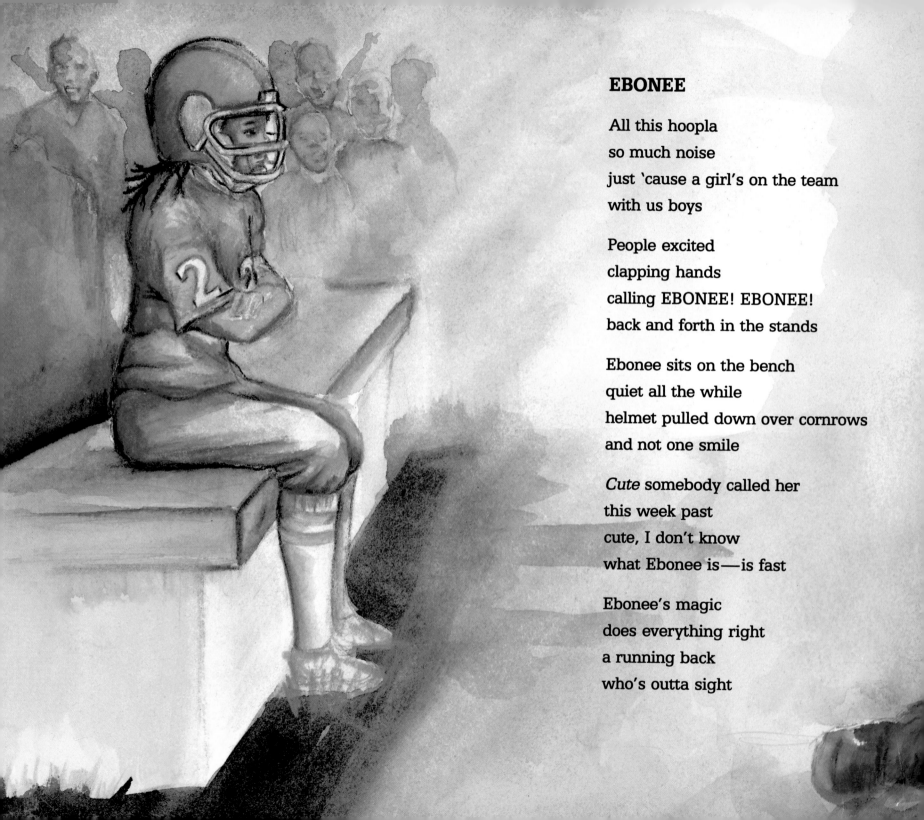

EBONEE

All this hoopla
so much noise
just 'cause a girl's on the team
with us boys

People excited
clapping hands
calling EBONEE! EBONEE!
back and forth in the stands

Ebonee sits on the bench
quiet all the while
helmet pulled down over cornrows
and not one smile

Cute somebody called her
this week past
cute, I don't know
what Ebonee is—is fast

Ebonee's magic
does everything right
a running back
who's outta sight

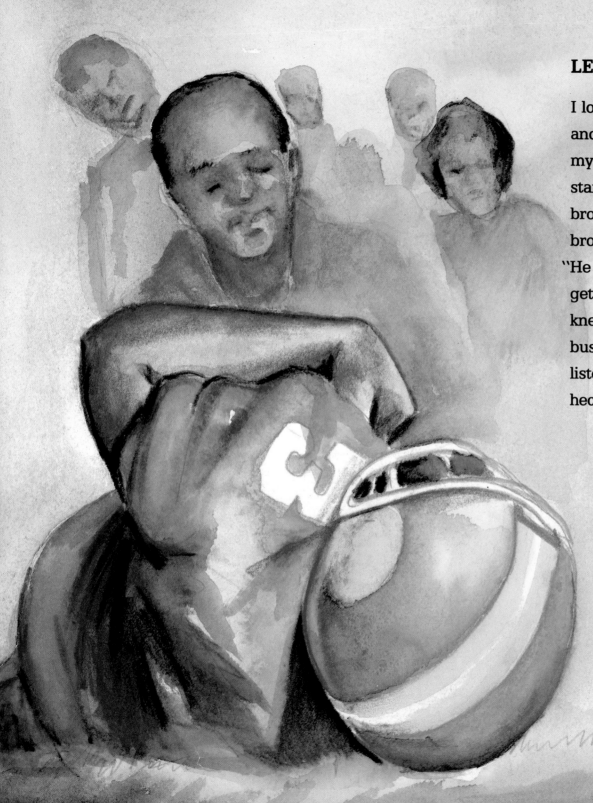

LEG BROKEN

I looked past my coaches
and what did I see
my father's eyes
staring straight at me
brown eyes worried
brown eyes mad
"He ain't old enough to play no football
getting hit from all around
knees messed up too early
busted open on the ground
listen here to what I say
heck no he can't play."

I looked past my coaches
and what did I see
my mother's eyes
staring straight at me
brown eyes praying
brown eyes proud
"Honey darling this is his dream
all his friends are on that team
I know he's young
but he's got pluck
and your old helmet
for luck."

I looked past my coaches
and what did I see
the eyes of my team
staring straight at me
brown eyes watching
brown eyes scared
saw two boys
bent on attack
slam my leg
to the side—and back
there I lay with a broken bone
arms outstretched
ball in the end zone

I looked at my coaches
and what did I see
all of them
staring straight at me
brown eyes brown eyes
brown eyes blue
victory and trouble
showing through
they lay me gently on the stretcher
tie the straps tight
whisper, "Boy, you caught that ball so good
held on and
ran it right."

I looked at myself
and what did I see
my leg all crumbly
near the knee
football's not an easy game
the boys who tackled me—I don't blame
both teams have a job to do
even if a nightmare comes true

COUSINS

He's decked out in white and green
baby face looking mean
his team's major man
they crush opponents at his command

I'm decked out in blue and gold
thin face looking cold
my team's major man
they crush opponents at my command

Two cousins
and neither can yield
facing one another
on a football field

Eleven men on his side
eleven on mine
two reputations
on the line

So we played
our big bad game
but the things that counted
remained the same

And it really would be
such a bore
to let you in
on the final score

What happened later
was the best of all
for two major men
cousins small

At a sleepover
that very night
we called a tie
in a major league
pillow fight

CHEERLEADERS

Swinging pom-poms
of blue and gold
they flash their colors
with control
they jump/shout/call
out loud
words that really jazz the crowd
bodies twirling, skirts swirling
first a circle
then a row
but at game's end
away they go

Voices mute
pom-poms still
they run toward the cars
at the top of the hill

PLAYOFF PIZZA

The pizza parlor
is the place to be
after a playoff victory
eating pepperoni
and extra cheese
we yell to one another
the game was a breeze
waving cups
of soda pop
we pose for pictures
on our way to the top
anchovies mushrooms
and sausage galore
Coach fussing
about errors
that almost ruined the score
black olives green peppers—and the sort
we can hardly eat all the stuff we bought
thin crusts thick crusts
deep dish too
for a happy team
dressed in gold and blue

CHAMPIONSHIP

Blue/Gold
Purple/Gold
weigh-in exciting
voices bold
we're 9 and 1
they're 10 and 0
two teams
ready to go

First quarter mistakes are many
both team coaches in a frenzy
the score when it bends
bends first to us
Purple/Gold quiet—no fuss
then they score a touchdown
and make the extra point
and you never heard noise
like the noise they made in this joint
then our Blue/Gold gets ahead
and tries to put the game to bed
we drive the ball
move it fast
our points pile up
and they can't get past
we outmatch them
play for play
and chase their perfect season away
27–7 is the official score
Blue/Gold folks
yelling More! More!

Champions now
we march
straight
across the field
helmets off
to a team
that tried
not to yield

But there's a Purple/Gold boy
I can't forget
helmet on
eyes wet
tears dripping
down his chin
His face
grabs something
from
my win

TROPHY

Tall treasure
you grew from the
hard soil
of chipped teeth
torn muscles
sprained ankles
broken legs
fractured fingers
4th down
field goals
sudden death
touchdowns
courage
unexpected
and surprising strength
from laps too long
pushups too many

Fancy golden football
gilded prize
you are the reason
at the end of a season
we are here
in this room
dressed up
excited
and
proud

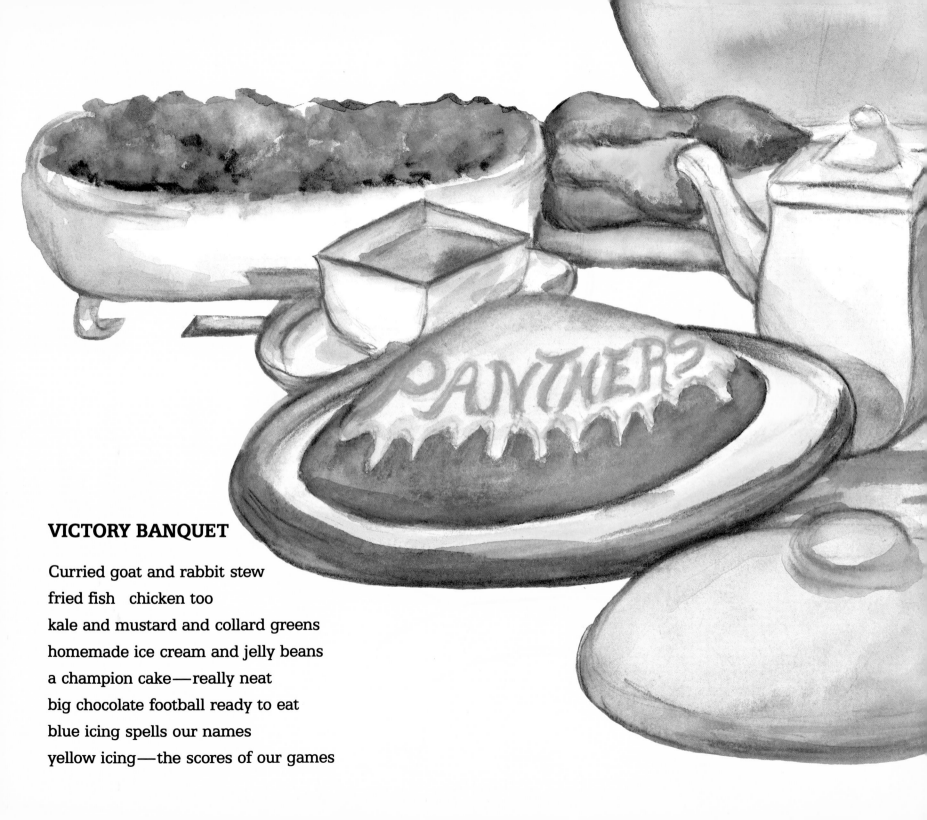

VICTORY BANQUET

Curried goat and rabbit stew

fried fish   chicken too

kale and mustard and collard greens

homemade ice cream and jelly beans

a champion cake—really neat

big chocolate football ready to eat

blue icing spells our names

yellow icing—the scores of our games

The team voted me—Teejay—master key

first a quarterback—now M.C.

when my speech begins

I thank family and coaches for our wins

Ebonee's words got started late

so much clapping for her—she's great

Bubba wearing his grandfather's tie

calls his grandpop a super guy

my grandma's swell too he said

she reads me stories when it's time for bed

Willie bragged he helped his Mama cook our pigeon peas and rice

and that's why he claims that dish was extra nice

Red is the boy all the girls like

but he's so shy he almost ran from the mike

Johnny—our safety—made us stand and cheer

for the championship we'll win—next year

Curried goat and rabbit stew

fried fish   chicken too

kale and mustard and collard greens

homemade ice cream and jelly beans

MOOSEHEART
ELEMENTARY
SCHOOL LIBRARY
60539

J
808.81
MAT

$12.56

Mathis, Sharon Bell
    Red dog blue fly
football poems

21259

ELEMENTARY LIBRARY
MOOSEHEART, ILLINOIS

DEMCO